The Sun's Special Blessing

BY SANDY WASSERMAN

ILLUSTRATED BY ANN D. KOFFSKY

PITSPOPANY

NEW YORK ◆ JERUSALEM ◆ LONDON

Published by PITSPOPANY PRESS
Text copyright © 2009 by Sandy Wasserman
Illustrations copyright © 2009 by Ann D. Koffsky
Editor – Sara Rosenbaum
Editorial and Production Director – Daniella Barak
Designed by Benjie Herskowitz

Hard Cover ISBN: 978-1-934440-92-6
French Flap ISBN: 978-1-934440-76-6

Printed in Israel

For
Kovi, Avrami, Tani and Racheli

Love, Aunt Ann

To my husband, Mel, who supports all my efforts,
my loving daughters, Michelle and Aliza,
and my granddaughter, Yael Brianna, my 'Sunshine!'

#6"**H**ave any of you ever made a *bracha*, a blessing, over the sun?" asked Mr. Jacobs, as he leaned against his desk.

Adam squirmed in his seat. Talia squinted at the sun through the frosty classroom window. She doodled in her notebook, thinking, *I never did.* Nobody raised a hand.

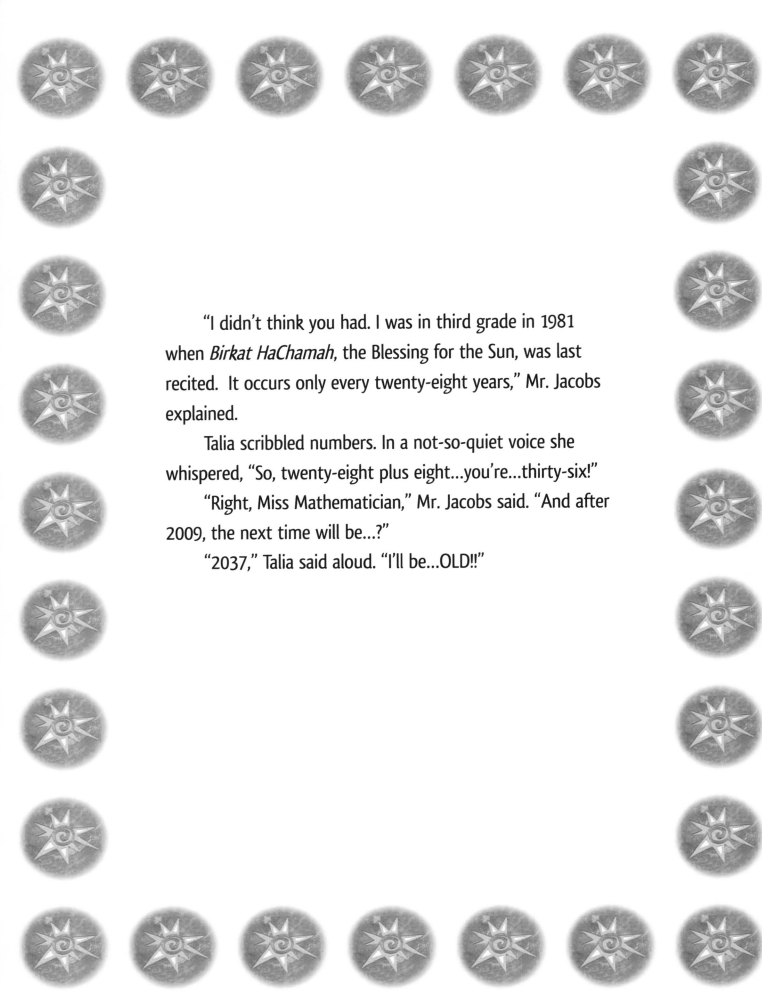

"I didn't think you had. I was in third grade in 1981 when *Birkat HaChamah*, the Blessing for the Sun, was last recited. It occurs only every twenty-eight years," Mr. Jacobs explained.

Talia scribbled numbers. In a not-so-quiet voice she whispered, "So, twenty-eight plus eight...you're...thirty-six!"

"Right, Miss Mathematician," Mr. Jacobs said. "And after 2009, the next time will be...?"

"2037," Talia said aloud. "I'll be...OLD!!"

"Have you ever wondered what people's lives were like years ago? Why did they bless the sun?" Mr. Jacobs asked.

"You mean that Jewish people have been blessing the sun every twenty-eight years since...forever!" said Adam. "Do we say the blessing because the sun gives heat and light, and helps plants to grow? That's a lot to bless God for. I'm happy when it's a sunny day. But why did they do it every twenty-eight years?"

"Ahh," Mr. Jacobs said. "Great questions! *Hashem*, God, created the sun on the fourth day of Creation. Even though the sun is in the sky daily, it's *only* in the *exact* spot as it was at Creation every twenty-eight years.

"Before modern times and today's technology, people praised God for the sun.

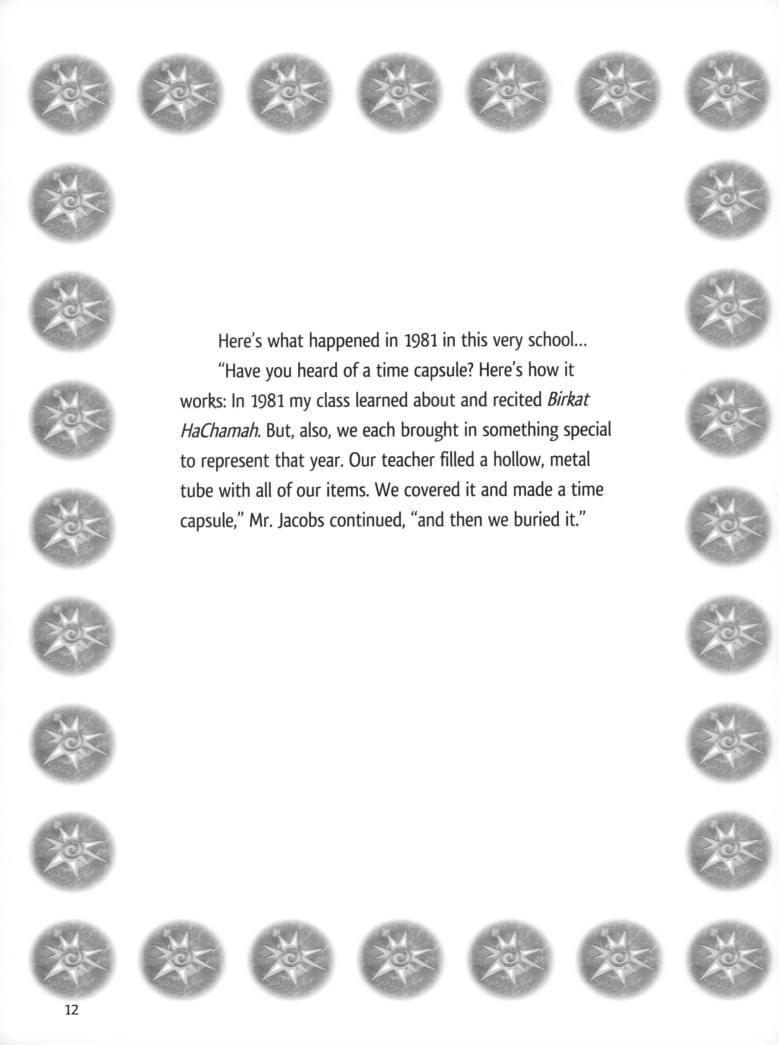

Here's what happened in 1981 in this very school…

"Have you heard of a time capsule? Here's how it works: In 1981 my class learned about and recited *Birkat HaChamah*. But, also, we each brought in something special to represent that year. Our teacher filled a hollow, metal tube with all of our items. We covered it and made a time capsule," Mr. Jacobs continued, "and then we buried it."

13

He raised a long-handled shovel over his head, and then removed several more from a large box. "This morning we'll take these shovels outside, near the flagpole, to dig up that old time capsule and examine what's inside. It's a matter of luck, but whoever is first to tap the time capsule with the shovel gets to keep what I included in it."

A roaring shout of, "YEAH!" went up all over the room and everyone flew to the door.

Mr. Jacobs led them to the spot he remembered burying the 1981 time capsule with his classmates. They took turns and began to dig and toss dirt.

"You're getting close! I have an excellent memory about this!" Mr. Jacobs shouted.

All of a sudden everyone heard a "CLINK!"

"I found it!" cried Talia. Everyone rushed over. Many hands scraped dirt, and tugged until... there it was – encrusted with earth – the 1981 time capsule!

Mr. Jacobs carefully removed it, brushing dirt from the metal case. Talia jumped, and Adam whooped.

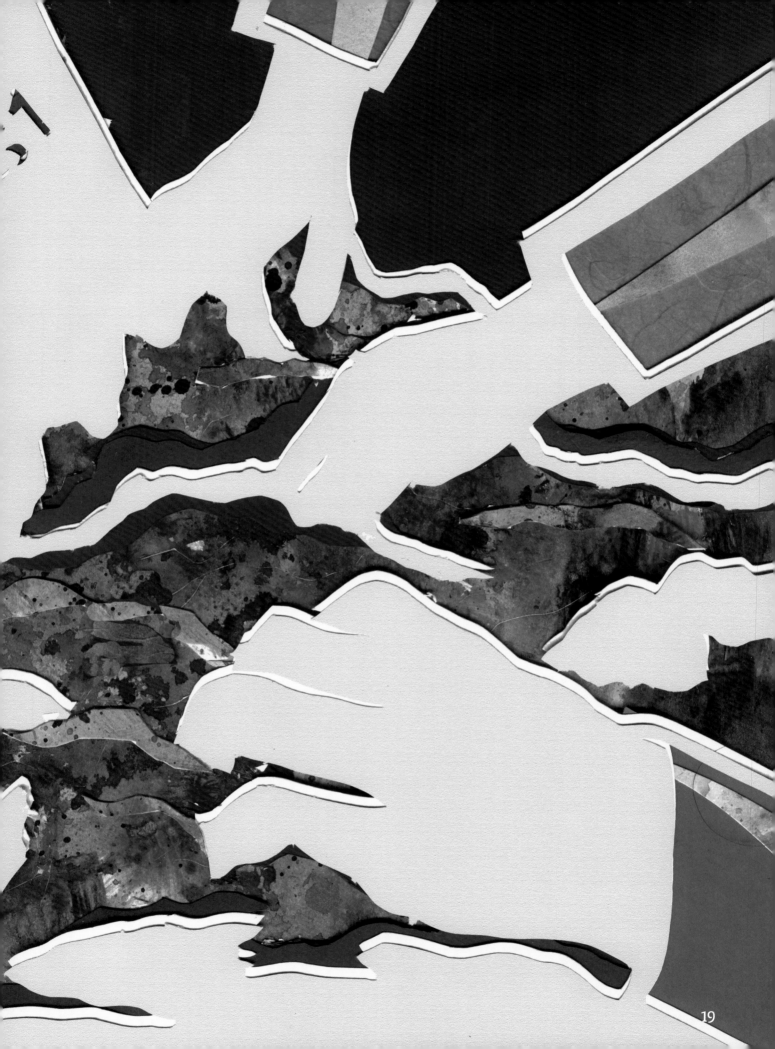

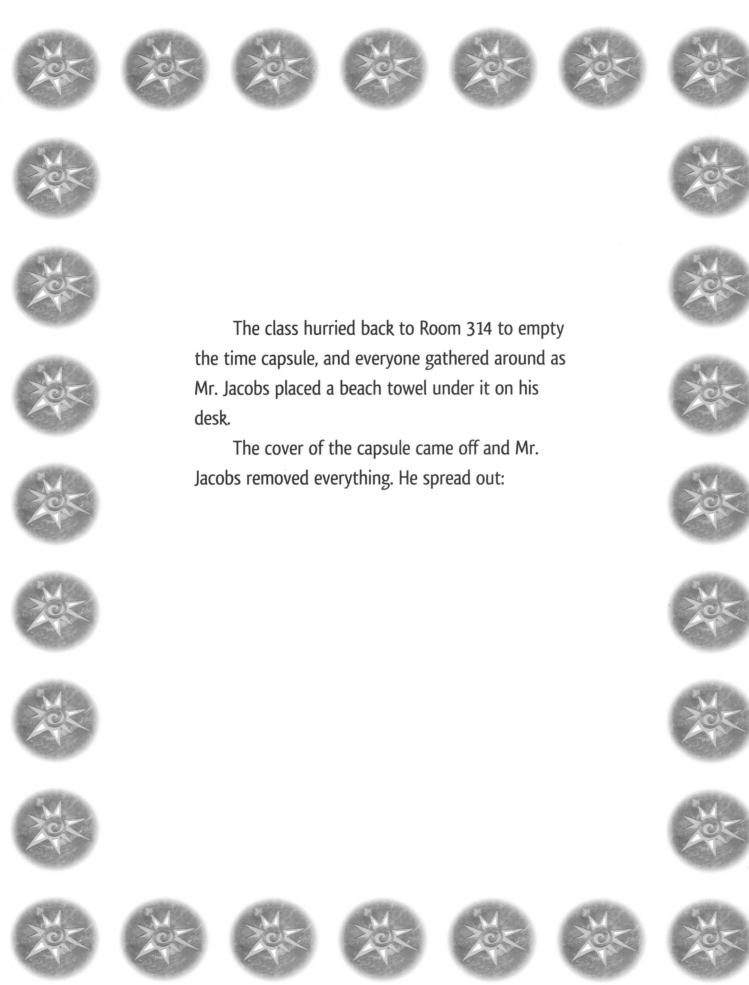

The class hurried back to Room 314 to empty the time capsule, and everyone gathered around as Mr. Jacobs placed a beach towel under it on his desk.

The cover of the capsule came off and Mr. Jacobs removed everything. He spread out:

· A movie poster from *Raiders of the Lost Ark*.

"Did it have superheroes in it?" asked Adam. "No," Mr. Jacobs said, "but it won for best movie."

· A small bag with five hard, metal cubes in them labeled '*Kugelach*'.

"Those are Israeli jacks," said Mr. Jacobs before anyone could ask. "They were popular in 1980. You throw them and catch them without a ball. Fun, but it hurts to grab them in your hand."

· A *New York Times* photo of former Presidents Jimmy Carter and Ronald Reagan.

The headline read, "Carter's Out, Reagan Inaugurated". "Hey, this stuff is history," Adam exclaimed. Mr. Jacobs smiled back.

· A magazine advertisement for a new 1981 Disney movie, *The Fox and the Hound*.

"I thought I knew all the Disney movies but I never heard of that one," said Adam.

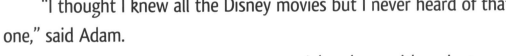

· A brochure with a giant game called '*Pac-Man*'.

"The *Pac-Man* picture looks like the first arcade videogame!" yelled Talia. Mr. Jacobs explained that *Pac-Man* was a new game in 1980 and kids played it on a HUGE video game player in stores. "It replaced a game called '*Pong*', which was a favorite of mine in elementary school, and was like ping-pong on a screen."

· A magazine advertisement for a new Apple computer and another for an IBM-PC. "They look so much bigger than our computer lab PCs," said Adam.

· A VHS movie tape with the name "3-2-1 Contact" on it.

"We still have some of those kinds of tapes at home. Weren't DVDs invented yet?" asked Talia. Mr. Jacobs shook his head, no. "3-2-1 Contact" was a popular kids' science show on television," he said.

· An article titled, "New Communication Tool – the *INTERNET*".

Everyone started laughing hard. "NEW! Are you kidding?" someone shouted. "Look at the photo of that suitcase-size PC!" Adam snickered

· Two plastic rectangles. One was named "Uncle Moishy." The other said "Debbie Friedman."

"Hey I think I heard of Uncle Moishy and Debbie Friedman music, but that's not a CD," Talia said. "You're right," Mr. Jacobs added. Before there were CDs, music was recorded on cassette tapes. If I can find a working cassette player, we can listen."

· A third cassette tape fell out with "Driedle Hannukah Game" written on it.

"Is that a song?" someone yelled. "Probably not," said Mr. Jacobs. "It must be a computer game written in an early computer language called 'BASIC'. We won't be able to view the game because we don't have that old technology any more. It's probably for an old TRS-80 computer."

· Two magazines bound in a frayed rubber band came out next.

One was named *Tom Thumb, Israeli Children's Magazine*, and the other was *The World Over – Olamaynu*. Both were dated December 1980.

"Let's have a look," said Adam. "Hey, Mr. Jacobs, I didn't know that there was real paper way back then." Mr. Jacobs tapped Adam on the head with the rolled up magazines, and gently placed them on the table. "I wish they were still published," Mr. Jacobs said. "You'd love them."

Clang! An envelope with stamps and coins slid out.

Mr. Jacob looked carefully and said, "Here are some five- and ten-agarot coins from Israel. That's before the current Israeli money called NIS, the New Israel Shekel, was put into use. And these fifteen-cent USA stamps are from the 1980 Winter Olympics held in Lake Placid, NY."

· A frayed, suede kippah with the faint outline of a painted figure on it.

Mr. Jacobs laughed. "I remember him – that's Papa Smurf!"

· There was a shiny eight-by-ten-inch photo of someone named John Lennon.

Talia yelled, "I know him! He was a singer called a 'Beatle'.

· A Rubik's Cube, with all the colors properly arranged.

"This brings back memories. That's what I included in the time capsule," said Mr. Jacobs, "this Rubik's Cube." Adam sputtered, "Is it really going to be Talia's? It's popular now. I *love* them!"

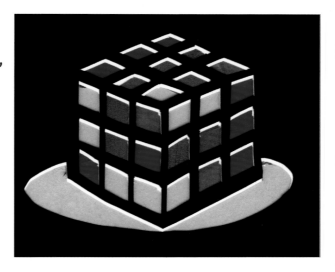

Everyone handled the contents of the time capsule for several minutes.

"Wow! Can I really take home your 1981 Rubik's Cube? For keeps?" asked Talia. "Thanks, Mr. Jacobs – cool!"

"You all might be wondering why we are looking through these objects," Mr. Jacobs said. "As I mentioned before, the *Birkat HaChamah* blessing stays the same every twenty-eight years. But do you think there are changes in the things you play with and care about today and these old items we removed?"

"Sure. But there have always been popular movies and toys and songs, haven't there, Mr. Jacobs?" Talia asked.

"We'll find out!" Mr. Jacobs continued. "I had so much fun filling the time capsule when I was a student," Mr. Jacobs answered. "Now since twenty-eight years have passed and it's time for this blessing again, I thought we'd do the 2009 version of this project. Except now we'll use this polyethylene container," and Mr. Jacobs brought a gigantic object over.

"This material is what NASA uses and we are going to use it for our 2009 time capsule so that our memorabilia won't disintegrate. And don't worry, this container has lots of space. But first things first," Mr. Jacobs continued. He distributed a booklet explaining the history of the blessing and the Hebrew calendar.

Talia glanced over it. There was a lot about math, her favorite subject!

ברכת החמה
1981
2009

"We make blessings all the time, in the synagogue and at home, expressing our wonder at God's creation," Mr. Jacobs reminded everyone. "Each month we make a *Rosh Chodesh* blessing for the moon. "We'll be busy between now and the 14th of the month of Nissan, learning about the blessing and also filling the time capsule. As we get closer to the actual date, we'll learn about the calendar and the sun's blessing."

And Mr. Jacobs chanted, "*Blessed are You, O Lord, our God, King of the Universe, Maker of Creation.*" In Hebrew it's, "*Baruch Atah Adonai Eloheinu Melech Ha'olam Oseh Ma'aseh Bereishit.*" "When will we say the blessing and bury the time capsule?" asked Talia.

"We'll make the *bracha* here in class in the morning during the first quarter of the day. Next we'll go outside with our trusty shovels and bury our own 2009 time capsule filled with our memorabilia. Usually we don't have class erev Pesach, but this is a superspecial year. So we'll be here on the 14th of Nissan – just for the morning – for *Birkat HaChamah*."

"What! An extra day of school!" Adam exclaimed. "But I guess it's okay this time – this will be fun."

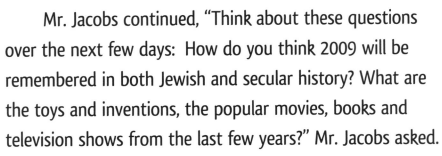

Mr. Jacobs continued, "Think about these questions over the next few days: How do you think 2009 will be remembered in both Jewish and secular history? What are the toys and inventions, the popular movies, books and television shows from the last few years?" Mr. Jacobs asked.

"Bring in something to include in our twenty-first century, polyethylene time capsule."

"Projects!" thought Talia. "I usually hate them, but this is an adventure!"

After Shabbat she fiddled with her "new" Rubik's Cube and started thinking about what she wanted to contribute to the new time capsule. She decided to include the book jacket from *Harry Potter and the Order of the Phoenix* and her *mini-Apollo 11 – 40th-Anniversary model*, celebrating the Apollo 11 Moon Landing. Her grandpa told her that Apollo 11 first landed on the moon in 1969 and he had just given her the model as a gift.

Talia's classmates looked around their houses, too, and chose their own items – a movie poster from *The Tale of Despereaux*, a *Horton Hears a Who* DVD, a Rick Recht CD, a photo of a 2009 BMW, a tiny, stuffed JingJing the Panda from the 2008 Summer Olympics in Beijing, an *Oy Baby* DVD, and photos of the Presidential Inauguration. Adam decided on a "2009-International Year of Astronomy" poster and a kippah from his brother's bar mitzvah, with "Parshat Bo, 6 Shevat/January 31, 2009," printed inside. Even Mr. Jacobs included items – a *Davka* catalog with all the latest software, and a CD celebrating Israel's 60th anniversary.

Talia was excited about reciting *Birkat HaChamah* right before Pesach. She hoped their time capsule would be discovered someday by new students, and she sighed as she drifted off to sleep.

I'm okay with giving up my new Apollo 11 model. It's worth it, she thought. *When I wake up I'm going to write a letter to include in the time capsule for this special year: "Shalom, dear students of the future..."*

Then she dreamed about the students in 2037 and pictured them excited to learn the special *Birkat HaChamah*, too, and amazed at the events of 2009.

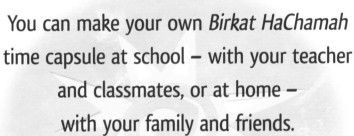

You can make your own *Birkat HaChamah* time capsule at school – with your teacher and classmates, or at home – with your family and friends. Bury it or hide it in a closet with a note that reminds you: DO NOT OPEN UNTIL APRIL 8, 2037 – for *BIRKAT HACHAMAH*.

ENDNOTES

Birkat HaChamah is Hebrew for "The Blessing of the Sun."

This is a special Hebrew prayer recited once every twenty-eight years – the period of the solar cycle. Jewish law stipulates that the prayer be said every 10,227 (28 times 365.25) days.

Once every twenty-eight years, the sun returns to the position it occupied when it was created at the beginning of the fourth day of creation.

When this occurs, a special prayer is recited acknowledging Hashem's might and His creation of the world. This blessing is known as the blessing of the sun, or *Birkat HaChamah*.

Every twenty-eight years, it is part of Jewish law (*Halacha*) to say *Birkat HaChamah* during the month of Nissan. The sun and moon were created on the fourth day, which was Tuesday at sundown until Wednesday at sundown. Therefore the beginning of the twenty-eight year cycle is always on a Wednesday. Wednesday is the fourth day of the week, and the blessing is recited in all years that are a multiple of twenty eight, plus one. We can say the blessing from the moment the upper arc of the sun first appears until the full disc of the sun is visible. The blessing only takes a few minutes to recite and is said after morning prayers, standing, and preferably with a *minyan*. Some authorities say that the blessing can be said until the end of the 3rd hour of the day; others say that it can be said until midday. *Birkat HaChamah* is always recited in the first year of the seven-year *shmita* (sabbatical) cycle (the seventh year is the sabbatical year when the land lies fallow and agricultural activity ceases). The following table lists the dates for *Birkat HaChamah*:

April 8, 1925 – Nissan 14, 5685

April 8, 1953 – Nissan 23, 5713

April 8, 1981 – Nissan 4, 5741

April 8, 2009 – Nissan 14, 5769

April 8, 2037 – Nissan 23, 5797

April 8, 2065 – Nissan 2, 5825

April 8, 2093 – Nissan 12, 5853

According to the Babylonian Talmud, tractate Berachot 59b, at these times the sun returns to the position that it was in when the universe was first created. The explanation is that if the year would be exactly 365.25 days, the sun's equinox times would be at the same time in the week every twenty-eight years. The tradition is that the sun was created in its spring equinox position, at the first hour of the night before the fourth day of Creation.

And Hashem made the two great lights: the greater light to rule the day, and the lesser light to rule the night and the stars. And Hashem placed them in the sky of the heavens to give light on the earth, and to rule over the day and over the night, and to divide the light from darkness; and Hashem saw that it was good. And it was evening and it was morning, a fourth day. (Genesis 1:16-19)

May it come to us and all Israel for good!